This royally important book belongs to:

———

_____

_____

For Grandma – GS

For Boo and Heidi – KC

NorthParadePublishing

©2015 North Parade Publishing Ltd.

4 North Parade,

Bath BA1 1LF. UK

www.nppbooks.co.uk

The Treehouse Princess

Princess Esme
and the Royal Giggles

Written by Grace Swanton
Illustrated by Kelly Caswell

NorthParadePublishing

Grandad held his spoon like a microphone. "It's 8.15 in the Fisher household," he said, "and I am joined by the delightful Miss Esme Fisher. Esme, what do you have planned for today?"

He held out the spoon for Esme to speak but she just giggled. **'Mr Newsreader'** was one of Esme's favourite games.

Esme wished Grandad
could come to stay more often.
He turned everything into a game.

 Brushing your teeth was a game.

Putting on socks was a game.

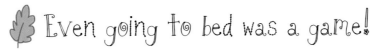 Even going to bed was a game!

One thing that was not a game, however, was mowing the lawn. While Grandad wheeled out their lawnmower, Esme climbed the rope ladder to her tree house. Inside, she did two very important things.

Important thing number 1: she closed the door behind her.

Important thing number 2: she opened a certain drawer and put a certain crown on her head.

Suddenly and quite magically, the inside of Esme's tree house transformed into a magnificent palace!

This time, Esme found herself in the huge Banquet Hall, where the King and Queen were having a long, leisurely sort of breakfast.

"Princess Esme," said the King of Cuddles, "how lovely to see you!"

The Queen of Hugs gave Esme a warm, cosy hug. "You're just in time," she said. "We're about to interview for our new butler. You can help us!"

Cuddledom Palace

WANTED!

(pretty please)

Butler to help run the Royal Palace

Must be:  cuddly

 helpful

 smartly dressed

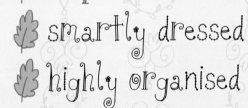 highly organised

The interviews began but the King and Queen were extremely fussy.
They made comments like:

"Too shiny."

"Too handsome."

"Too muscly."

"Too... pink."

After the hundredth interview, the King gave a long sigh. "That was the last one," he said.

"Oh, Cuddles!" said the Queen. "Were we too picky? Perhaps we should start again? What does Her Little Highness think?"

Princess Esme thought for a moment.

"I think a butler should always be funny," she said. "Even the King and Queen need a giggle every now and again!"

So the King of Cuddles called everyone back. This time, they asked the butlers to make them laugh.

"Ha," said the Queen.

"Ho," said the King.

"Teehee," said Princess Esme.

But they were only the tiniest of laughs. None of the butlers were as funny as Esme had hoped.

Suddenly, a new candidate burst into the room. He ran over to the King and removed the King's slippers.

"Excuse me!" began the King, "I, aho... aha... aho-ho-ho-haha!" Then he hooted and howled until his cheeks turned purple.

The Queen sniggered and snorted until her crown toppled off.

And Esme laughed at them all.

Finally, the King gave Esme the royal nod. She shook the man's hand and said, "Thank you for giving us the royal giggles. Would you like to be our new butler?"

"Yes!" beamed the new butler. "I would!"

"Could you tell us your name, kind chap?" asked the King.

"Tickles," he replied. "My name is Tickles."

And the royal giggles struck again!

Just then, Esme heard a loud yelp. She ran to the door and looked outside. Grandad had run over the hosepipe with the lawnmower and was getting soaked! "That would make the King and Queen laugh," she thought.

Esme turned to tell them but the palace had vanished.

Esme took off her crown and put it back in the second-biggest drawer. As she climbed down from her tree house, she thought about the King's ticklish feet and giggled.

The little bell on the tree house jingled, as if it were giggling too.

Colour in your own magical tree house.